THE CHURCH MICE AT BAY

Graham Oakley

ATHENEUM   NEW   YORK

Also by Graham Oakley

The Church Mouse
The Church Cat Abroad
The Church Mice and the Moon
The Church Mice Spread Their Wings
The Church Mice Adrift

One July morning in Wortlethorpe, a few of the vicar's friends gathered outside the vicarage to see him off on his summer holidays. When the coach had gone, they chatted about the new curate who was coming to take over for the next few weeks. There wasn't much to say because no one had yet met him, but they all hoped he would be a nice quiet young chap like the one they'd had last year.

He wasn't.

But Humphrey, the schoolmouse, was very impressed with him. The rest of the church mice and Sampson, the church cat, reserved judgement.

Later, they all went back to the vicarage to see how the new curate was settling in. Humphrey was even more impressed. Everybody else was non-committal.

The next morning Sampson and the mice went into the churchyard and spent the whole day sunbathing. When they returned to the vestry at tea time, they found that during their absence the curate had made a few changes. Even Humphrey wasn't too keen on these but everybody agreed that given time a chap's eyes can get used to anything.

After tea, the mice usually sat under the surplice cupboard and listened to the choir practising nice hymns like *From Greenland's Icy Mountains*. It seemed that the curate had made a few more changes. Humphrey wasn't too keen on these, either, but they all agreed that given time a chap's ears can get used to anything.

Next day brought the worst change of all. Every Friday, by a long-standing gentleman's agreement with the vicar, their weekly allowance of cheese in payment for services rendered was brought to the vestry. Now, late on Friday evening, there before their very eyes, plain for all to see, was absolutely nothing. They were thunderstruck, and this time they all agreed that eyes and ears were one thing but a chap's stomach was sacred.

So they sent a deputation across to the vicarage to protest to the curate.

Unfortunately he was terrified of mice and their visit made him quite hysterical. He told Sampson that it was a church cat's duty to *catch* church mice not to *hob nob* with them and if Sampson didn't do his duty he'd find a *proper* cat who would.

Sampson's vow never to harm mice had given him a lot of trouble in the past but never as much as this. The vestry was a dreary place that night until Arthur, who had a practical turn of mind, thought up a plan. It was very simple. When the curate next appeared Sampson would pretend to be catching the last few mice. After that they would hide and the curate would think they had all been caught.

The plan worked well. It didn't solve the cheese problem of course but the mice were prepared to change their diet until the vicar came home. But from Sampson's point of view, the plan had obvious drawbacks, and he infuriated the mice by thinking up a new one.

It was an even simpler plan than Arthur's and it had to do with the curate's mouse-phobia. They would frighten him so much that he would run away and never come back.

It would have worked, too, if the mayor hadn't been driving past in his brand new Rolls-Royce.

Sampson and the mice got all the blame, of course.
The mayor was furious with them and shouted
things like "vermin" and "fleabag" and told them
that it was the likes of them who were "Tarnishing
the Noble Name of Wortlethorpe in the Eyes of
All Mankind."

After all that, they thought they had better lie low for a time so they went and rummaged on the municipal rubbish dump. Then, after a couple of hours, they went back to the church to see if the trouble had blown over.

It was worse than ever.

In fact things were so bad that they were even willing to listen to Humphrey. He said that speaking as a chap who kept his Finger on the Pulse of the Times, he thought what was needed was a Protest March. As no one had any other ideas, they decided to give it a try.

They had chosen a good time because that afternoon the curate was giving his first garden party.

The mice thoroughly enjoyed the march and even Sampson entered fully into the spirit of things.

That night they had to camp out in the lychgate because the new church cat was sleeping in the vestry. But they were happy because now the mayor knew all about their cause and was sure to do something about it soon.

He did do something . . .

. . . first thing next morning.

Whether the mice escaped through Divine Intervention, as Humphrey claimed . . .

. . . or by sheer fluke, as Arthur claimed, no one will ever know.

But escape they did, and they set off to look for Sampson. Finding him didn't prove too difficult . . .

. . . but getting him out of the cage under the noses of all the other cats was another matter.

Humphrey said it was a pity he had never studied hypnotism because then he would have put the cats to sleep, and Arthur replied sarcastically that it was a pity that *he* had never studied magic because then he could have made the cats disappear. As it was, they would just have to stoop to trickery.

When Sampson was out of the cage, Humphrey tied the door shut with a knot of his own invention called "The Humphrey Patent Double-Reefed Running Sheepshanked Granny Knot MkII" which he personally guaranteed absolutely unslippable. It slipped.

And the sight of all those cats going free was more than any dog could take sitting down.

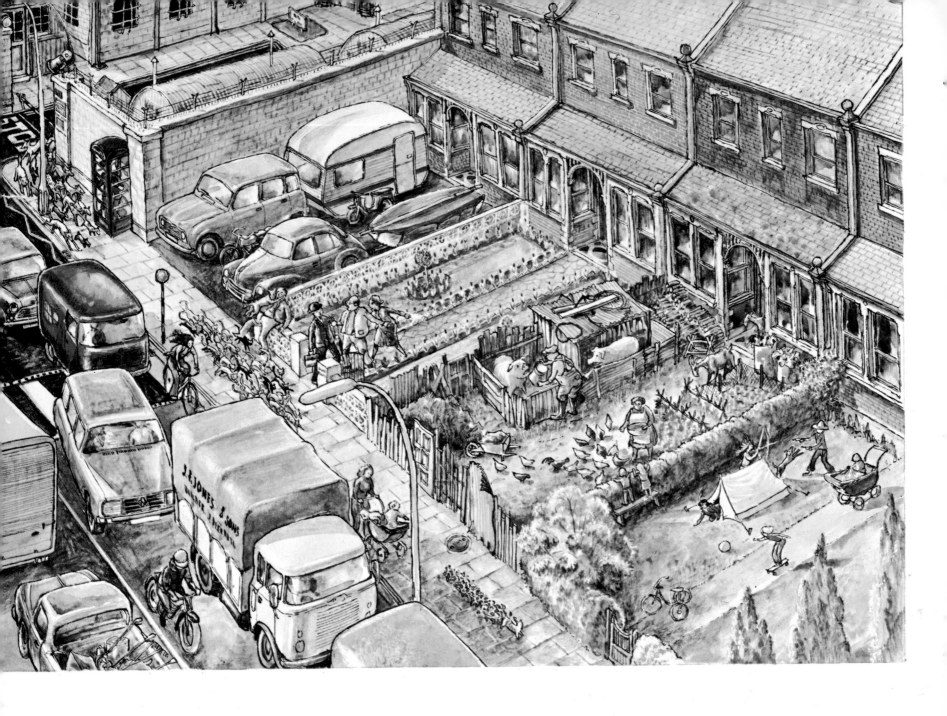

Sampson first realized they were being pursued when they were getting near the vicarage.

. . . he had left the bathroom door open.

Inside the vicarage, the curate was taking a bath,
and as he wanted to listen to Groovy Grumbold's
Rock Roundup on Radio Wortlethorpe . . .

That . . .

. . . was a mistake.

Sampson and the mice were now on home ground and soon found a hiding place.

But outside, there was no hiding place for the curate. That day, at enormous expense, the New European Tea-cosy and Muff Wing of the Wortlethorpe Museum was being opened, and to mark the occasion a procession was taking place headed by the most important and distinguished people in the whole county . . .

. . . and the curate met them all.

The meeting was not fruitful. He resigned on the spot.

The curate decided to leave next morning. Wortlethorpe, he said, was not his scene. A telegram was sent off to the vicar at Bognor and he gladly cut short his holiday.

He immediately gave Sampson six tins of New Fat-Kat with Added Biopolychlorodiamin for Personal Freshness, and the mice received double rations of cheese because they had all had to put up with so much.

Soon the choir was practising *From Greenland's Icy Mountains* again, and the paintings in the vestry were covered with a nice shade of buff paint which looked as if it had been on the walls for twenty-five years before it was even dry.

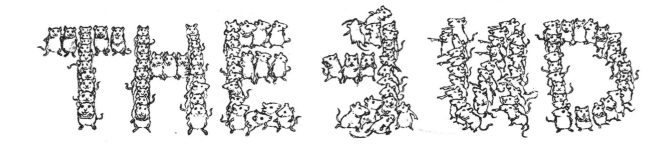